THE TOOT FAIRY

MARK HUFFMAN

Illustrated By
Dawn Davidson

BROWN BOOKS KIDS

The Toot Fairy

Brown Books Kids
Dallas / New York
www.BrownBooksKids.com
(972) 381-0009

A New Era in Publishing®

Publisher's Cataloging-In-Publication Data

Names: Huffman, R. M., author. | Davidson, Dawn, 1977– illustrator.
Title: The toot fairy / Mark Huffman ; illustrated by Dawn Davidson.
Description: Dallas ; New York : Brown Books Kids, (2021) | Interest age level: 006–008. | Summary: "When it's time for Jessa the fairy to proclaim what kind of fairy she wants to be, she accidentally says "toot fairy" instead of "tooth fairy!" Now she'll be in charge of collecting all the toots from all the butts in the world. This is not exactly what she had in mind"––Provided by publisher.
Identifiers: ISBN 9781612544861
Subjects: LCSH: Fairies––Juvenile fiction. | Flatulence––Juvenile fiction. | CYAC: Fairies––Fiction. | Flatulence––Fiction.
Classification: LCC PZ7.1.H797 To 2021 | DDC (E)––dc23

ISBN 978-1-61254-486-1
LCCN 2020912921

Printed in the United States
10 9 8 7 6 5 4 3 2 1

For more information or to contact the author, please go to
www.TheHuffmanLetters.com.

Dedication
For Asher, Cole, Clara, and Sophie

Acknowledgments

Thanks to my wife, my four kids, my dad, my numerous nieces and nephews and coworkers and friends who served as test audiences, the excellent and talented people at Brown Books who turned my poem into a book, and above all Jesus Christ, Who I trust can use even a children's book about toots for His glory.

In Fairyland, fairies can choose what to do.

They can go to the fountain where wishes come true.

Some fairies say "rainbow"
to shine after showers.

Some fairies say "garden"
to live among flowers.

If you ask little Jessa,
she'd tell you the truth:

From the time
she was young,

she had planned
to say "tooth."

What a wonderful thing for a fairy to do!

To collect all the teeth that small children outgrew

How delighted they'd be

when they found in their beds

Coins for each little chomper

that fell from their heads!

The day finally arrived.
Little Jess was excited
To start the career
upon which she'd decided.

She stepped to the fountain and threw in a coin
And got ready to speak out the job she would join.

But when that moment came
to say what she would be,
She pronounced, to her horror,
the "t–h" as "t"!

TOOT!

She had clearly said "toot"!
Everybody had heard!

All her plans went kaput
with one misspoken word!

In a cloud of green fog,
a strange fairy appeared.
He had long, golden robes
and a wispy, white beard.

"My name's Poobums the Pungent,"

he said with a bow.

"You'll be working with me
in a job that starts now!

"This is one of our more, um, forgotten careers. There's not been a toot fairy for hundreds of years!

From the world's greatest queen!

Every person around you
is tooting like nuts,

Shooting gross—smelling gasses
from out of their butts.

"Whether silent
but deadly
or shockingly LOUD,

Every toot disappears, for it's just a brief cloud.

"So you've got to be nimble.
You've got to be quick.

Because toots
don't last long,
but they're coming out thick.

Why, statistically speaking,
there's billions a day,
So you see why this job
is all work and no play

"For it's your task, young fairy,
to find every one.
It's not glamorous work,
but it needs to be done.

Here, these
magical goggles
can help you to tell.

Also, sometimes there's noise,
Plus a terrible smell!"

Jessa said, "I like *teeth*," in a sad, quiet voice, "But I'll try very hard, though it's not my first choice."

Poobums stopped. He could see that poor Jess was in pain
So he stroked his white beard, and he tried to explain.

And a toot's like a tooth,

for they both possess mass,

Except one's made of dentin,

the other of gas.

"Both are one of a kind!
Custom-ordered! Handmade!
And when kids push 'em out,
they deserve to get paid!

"So, we take out our coin,
whether quarter or dime,
And we wait for the toot.
Then, at just the right time,

When we feel the explosions
come out their back doors,
Put the coin in their pants!
Stuff it right down the drawers!"

To her credit, sweet Jessa
was barely dejected,

Though 'twasn't the work
she had ever expected.

Instead, she was filled
with a strong sense of duty.
She'd find every toot!
She would sniff every booty!

And that's what she did,
and she'll do it for years:
Trading cash for the vapors
expelled from our rears.

If there's change
in your pants
after tooting,
don't fear.

It's just Jess,
hard at work,
making quarters
appear.

About the Author

MARK HUFFMAN writes about our shared human experiences, which is a pretentious way to say that he writes about toots and bottoms and food. He prepared for writing children's books by spending much of his early life as an actual child. Unlike other children's authors he might name who have spuriously claimed the title, he is a real doctor. He lives with his family in Texas.

About the Illustrator

DAWN DAVIDSON is a freelance artist in Winter Garden, Florida. A lover of great children's literature, she is inspired by the classical illustrators of the past and strives to achieve a sense of timelessness by mimicking traditional media in her digital work. Combining classical drawing skills, vibrant color use, and a sense of playful whimsy to create memorable characters and humorous compositions, she enjoys nothing more than to bring a story to life through beautiful, engaging art. She loves family, travel, Celtic mythology, period and fantasy costuming, and dreaming of retiring to a mountain cottage in a state that has seasons.